The Gingerbread Man

Rewritten by Madge Tovey

Illustrated by Wayne Andreason

A little old man and a little old woman lived in a cozy cottage. The cottage was on a farm near the woods.

2

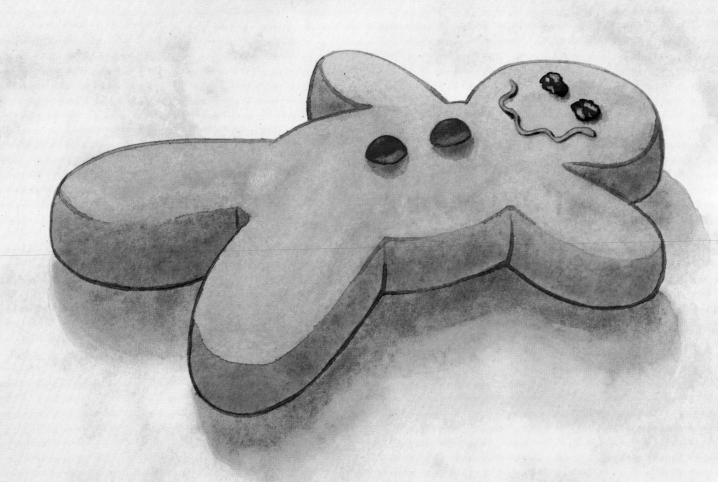

The little old woman could bake the most delicious things.
One day she baked a gingerbread man. He had dark raisin eyes,
a pink frosting mouth, and fat gumdrop buttons.

She popped him into the oven
and waited till the delicious smell
filled the kitchen.

"I'll just take a peek to see if he's done," she said. She opened the oven. Out hopped the gingerbread man!

He ran across the kitchen and out the door. "Stop, stop, Gingerbread Man!" cried the little old woman. But the gingerbread man just laughed.

"Run, run as fast as you can. You can't catch me, I'm the gingerbread man!"

7

He ran down the path and into the garden.
The little old man stopped hoeing and cried,
"Stop, stop, Gingerbread Man!" But the
gingerbread man just laughed.

"Run, run as fast as you can.
You can't catch me, I'm the gingerbread man!
I ran away from the little old woman.
And I can run away from you, I can!"

He ran through the garden and into the
pasture. A cream-colored cow stopped chewing
and cried, "Stop, stop, Gingerbread Man!"
But the gingerbread man just laughed.

10

"Run, run as fast as you can.
You can't catch me, I'm the gingerbread man!
I ran away from the little old woman.
I ran away from the little old man.
And I can run away from you, I can!"

11

He ran through the pasture and down the lane. A heavy old horse, who was leaning on the fence, cried, "Stop, stop, Gingerbread Man!" But the gingerbread man just laughed.

"Run, run as fast as you can. You can't catch me, I'm the gingerbread man! I ran away from the little old woman. I ran away from the little old man. I ran away from the cream-colored cow. And I can run away from you, I can!"

He ran down the lane and came to a stream.
A furry-tailed fox looked out of his den and
cried, "Stop, stop, Gingerbread Man!" But the
gingerbread man just laughed.

"Run, run as fast as you can.
You can't catch me, I'm the
gingerbread man!"

"I ran away from the little old woman.
I ran away from the little old man.
I ran away from the cream-colored cow.
I ran away from the heavy old horse.
And I can run away from you, I can!"

16

The fox smiled and said, "I don't like to eat gingerbread men, but if you hop onto my back, I will carry you across the stream."

The gingerbread man hopped onto the fox's back, and the fox waded into the stream. The water came up higher and higher. "Hop onto my head to keep dry," said the fox.

The gingerbread man hopped onto the fox's head. Soon the water came up higher and higher. "Hop onto my nose to keep dry," said the fox.

The gingerbread
man hopped onto
the fox's nose.

The fox's nose went twitchety twitch.
The gingerbread man flipped into the air.
The fox caught him with his teeth.
Snip, snap, crunch! The fox ate him
up with a munch!

"Gingerbread men are made to be eaten," said the fox with a sly smile.